The Green Musician

Retold by Mahvash Shahegh

Illustrated by Claire Ewart

❖Wisdom Tales❖

Once upon a time in the land of Persia, there lived a king named Khosrow. He was very wealthy and his palace was full of colorful rugs and other rich decorations. Everything the king and his guests ate was plentiful and delicious. The large palace gardens were overflowing with rare flowers, trees, and songbirds.

Now, King Khosrow loved music and song. The very best musician and singer in the land was chosen to live at the king's palace. His name was Sarkash and he would sing beautiful songs for the king and his court. Of course, every singer in the land wanted to sing for the king and live at the palace. However, only the best would ever do so.

In a distant part of the kingdom there lived another singer and musician whose name was Barbad. He, too, wished to become the king's favorite musician and live at the palace. In that way, he could send money back home to help his family, as was the custom in those times.

And so Barbad left home and traveled
to the king's city.

When Sarkash learned that Barbad had come to the city to see the king, he was filled with jealousy. Sarkash had heard about Barbad's great talent. He was afraid the king would prefer Barbad over him. So, with the help of his friends in the court, Sarkash delayed the meeting.

For almost a year, Barbad could not see the king.
Barbad, however, did not give up.

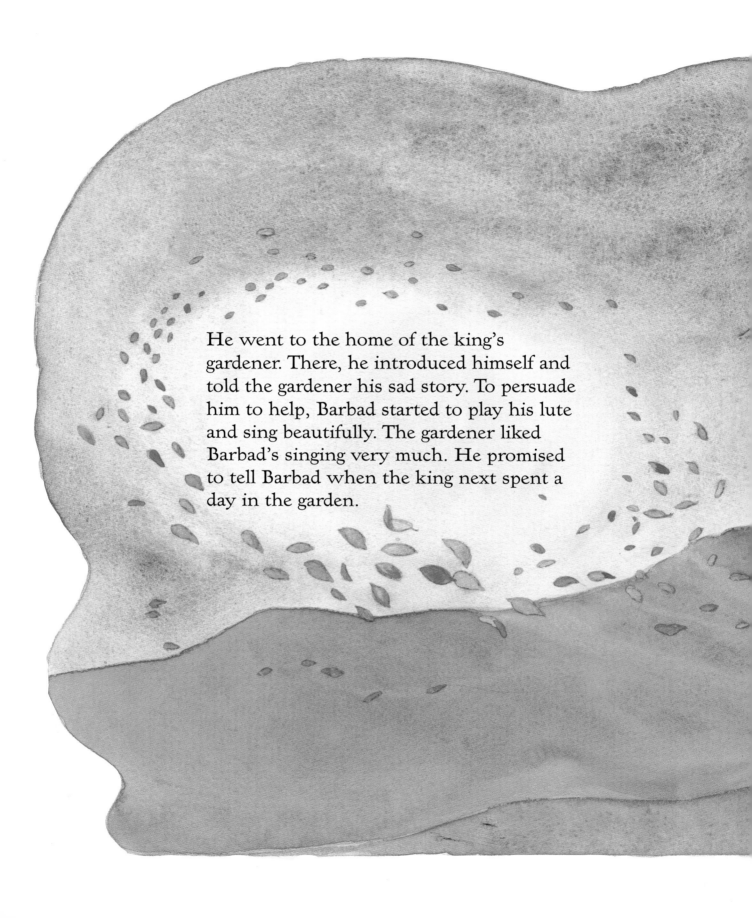

He went to the home of the king's
gardener. There, he introduced himself and
told the gardener his sad story. To persuade
him to help, Barbad started to play his lute
and sing beautifully. The gardener liked
Barbad's singing very much. He promised
to tell Barbad when the king next spent a
day in the garden.

First, Barbad had to wait until the arrival of spring.

By then the flowers were in full bloom and the trees had become green again. Finally, the king decided it was time to visit his garden.

When the gardener found out about the king's visit, he quickly sent a messenger to inform Barbad. The young musician would not miss this chance for anything in the world!

So the promised day arrived and Barbad hurried to the palace. He was dressed all in green and had colored his instrument in green, too. The gardener secretly let Barbad into the garden through a special gate.

Barbad quickly climbed a tall tree and hid himself and his musical instrument among its leaves. He did this in such a clever way that nobody could tell him or his instrument apart from the tree.

Soon after, the king and his court arrived. They touched the full-bloomed flowers and smelled the sweet-scented plants. With silent gratitude, they admired nature's beauty. Then the king and all the others sat down to eat, drink, and enjoy themselves.

As night fell over the garden, Barbad
picked up his instrument and started to
sing. Everyone there, including the king,
was completely entranced by the beauty of
the music and song. Yet, no one could tell
where the mysterious sound came from.

When the song finished, King Khosrow ordered his men to find the source of this heavenly music. They searched the entire garden, but found nothing. Perhaps, they said, the flowers, trees, and songbirds had all joined together to sing in honor of the king and his good deeds.

The king and his court returned to their festivities. Suddenly, another beautiful song emerged from the darkness of the garden. This time the king did not wait for the song to finish. He ordered his servants to begin searching immediately. They looked everywhere. Alas, all they found were chirping birds!

After the search was over, the king resumed
his dinner with friends and family. But,
again, they heard angelic music and song. It
was yet another melody coming mysteriously
out of the air.

This time the king was determined to find the source of the music. He called out in a loud voice, "I do not know if it comes from an angel or a demon. Yet, surely this beautiful voice could not be produced by a demon!" The king added, "I will give rich rewards to whoever has made these songs!"

When Barbad heard the king's promise, he climbed down the tree. King Khosrow was surprised to see a green musician approaching him!

He asked Barbad to tell him more about himself. So Barbad told the king how he had tried to meet him. Barbad explained that Sarkash was jealous of him and had kept him from meeting the king.

Hearing this, the king became angry with Sarkash. He made Barbad the court's new musician and singer and he told Sarkash to leave the palace.

Barbad became famous all over the kingdom and lived happily ever after in the court of the king. Today, people still tell the story of Barbad the green musician. They speak of how nothing could stop him from pursuing his dreams.

Background

This is a story retold and adapted for children from the *Shāhnāmeh*, or "Book of Kings," written in around 1,000 CE by the Persian poet Ferdowsī. The main character in the story, Bārbad (pronounced Bawr-bad), is a true historical character who was the most talented and skilled musician of his time. He was the minstrel-poet of the court of the Sassanid king, Khosrow Parvēz (591-628 CE). *The Green Musician* depicts his visit with the king and the way he competes with his rival, Sarkash, for the position of chief minstrel at the king's court.

There are several stories that show how much the king appreciated Bārbad's talent, how fond he was of his music, and how much he was influenced by Bārbad's counsel. Legend has it that whenever the king disfavored a courtier, they would approach Bārbad to mediate with the king for pardon.

Another story fully depicts Bārbad's talent and skill. While he was taking a short break during one of the king's banquets, a colleague altered the tuning of Bārbad's lute out of jealousy. When he returned, Bārbad realized the sabotage, but continued his faultless performance since he knew the king did not like instruments to be tuned in his presence. Only at the end of the banquet was the king informed of Bārbad's deceitful colleague.

Bārbad composed verses and sang them at the state banquet during the festivities, especially at Nowrūz (the Iranian New Year). He was so prolific that he composed a song for each day of the year. Alas, out of all these songs only one has survived.

There are varying accounts about the end of Bārbad's life. Some relate that upon the king's death, Bārbad was so distressed that he left the court and burned all his instruments. Others claim that Bārbad was poisoned by his rival, Sarkash. Whatever the case, Bārbad's name continues to live on in history to this day.

About the Author and Illustrator

Mahvash Shahegh is an author, educator, librarian, researcher, and translator who taught at Johns Hopkins University until her recent retirement. She earned a PhD in Persian language and literature in Iran with a dissertation on "The Trace of Fairies in Persian Stories and Literature." Inspired by her own grandchildren, her goal as a writer is to share the beauty of Persian culture with children all over the world. She is the author of a two-volume Persian language book for college students, co-authored with two of her colleagues, titled *Learning Persian*. She lives outside of Baltimore, MD.

Claire Ewart is an award-winning author and illustrator of children's books. Her most recent book is *The Olive Tree* by Elsa Marston. In addition to illustrating books by such well-known authors as Tomie dePaola and Paul Fleischman, she has also written and illustrated several of her own books, including *One Cold Night*, *The Giant*, and *Fossil*. Claire's books have been recommended by the *Field Guide for Parenting*, *Booklinks*, and *PBS Teacher Source*, while her work as an illustrator has been included on Best Book lists from *School Library Journal* and *Parent's Magazine*. Her work has also appeared on the PBS television shows *Reading Rainbow* and *Storytime*. Claire lives in Fort Wayne, IN.